To Barbara Firth
M. W.

To Morwenna
B. F.

Text copyright © 2007 by Martin Waddell
Illustrations copyright © 2007 by Barbara Firth

First U.S. edition 2007

Library of Congress Cataloging-in-Publication Data is available.

Library of Congress Catalog Card Number 2006046286

ISBN 978-0-7636-3310-3

2 4 6 8 10 9 7 5 3 1

Printed in Singapore

This book was typeset in Golden Cockerell.

The illustrations were done in watercolor and pencil.

Candlewick Press
2067 Massachusetts Avenue
Cambridge, Massachusetts 02140

visit us at www.candlewick.com

Bee Frog

Martin Waddell   illustrated by Barbara Firth

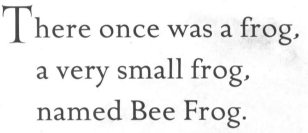

There once was a frog,
a very small frog,
named Bee Frog.

Bee played all day with her sisters and brothers.
They played
Can't Catch Me, Frog,
Frog-Hop,
Frog-Plop, and . . .

I'm Not a Frog—
I'm a
DRAGON.

Then Mom Frog called them in.

"I'm Bee Frog the Dragon,"
Bee told Mom Frog.
"Yes, Bee, that's nice,"
croaked Mom Frog.

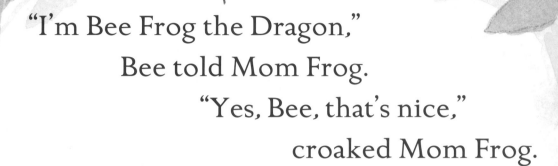

"I'm not nice — I'm a dragon," croaked Bee.
"Yes, dear, I see," croaked Mom Frog.

"I'm Bee Dragon,"
Bee told Dad Frog.
"Be quiet, Bee,"
croaked Dad Frog.

"I'm a very fierce dragon!" croaked Bee.
"So I see," said Dad Frog without looking at Bee.

"I'm Bee Dragon,"
Bee told Grandma Frog.
But Grandma Frog was fast asleep on her lily
and she didn't hear Bee.

"No one listens to me!"
croaked Bee Frog.

"I'm hopping off!"
croaked Bee Frog.

"I'm hopping off
and I'm not coming back,

not ever,
not *never*!"

Hop!

Hop!

Hop!

Hop!

Hop!

Hop!

Hop!

Bee Frog landed on a dark stone,
with reeds all around it.

This is good! thought Bee Frog.
I like it! thought Bee.
I love it! thought Bee.

And she made dragon noises
all by herself.

I'm Bee Dragon! thought Bee.
I'm Bee Dragon, the really fierce dragon! thought Bee.
Everyone's SCARED of Bee Dragon!
thought Bee.

Then . . .

I wonder if dragons get lonely, thought Bee.

Mom and Dad Frog
came looking for Bee.

"Bee Dragon! Bee Dragon!"
they croaked.

Bee sat very still, until they
were almost beside her.
And then . . .

CROAK!

Bee ambushed her mommy and daddy.

"We've found you,
Bee Dragon!"
croaked Mom and Dad Frog.

"I'm not really a dragon,"
croaked Bee.

"Well . . ."
croaked Mom Frog.

"You look like a very
fierce dragon to me!"
said Dad Frog.

"I'm not! I'm your BEE!"
croaked Bee Frog.

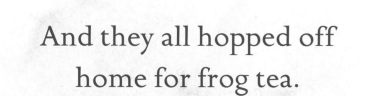

And they all hopped off
home for frog tea.